Disney's
A Winnie the Pooh First Reader
Pooh's Hero Party

by Isabel Gaines
ILLUSTRATED BY STUDIO ORLANDO

DISNEY PRESS

NEW YORK

Printed in the United States of America.

Based on the Pooh stories by A. A. Milne (copyright The Pooh Properties Trust).

First Edition

3 5 7 9 10 8 6 4 2

This book is set in 18-point Goudy.

Library of Congress Catalog Card Number: 98-86075

ISBN: 0-7868-4270-9

For more Disney Press fun, visit www.DisneyBooks.com

Pooh's Hero Party

Disney's
Winnie the Pooh First Readers

Pooh's
Hero Party

It was a stormy day

in the Hundred-Acre Wood.

The wind blew very hard.

So hard that it blew

Owl's house down.

Christopher Robin, Eeyore,

and Rabbit came

to see the damage.

"When a house looks like that,"

said Eeyore, "it is time

to find another one.

Owl, I will find a new house for you."

The stormy day turned into

a stormy night.

The Hundred-Acre Wood flooded.

Christopher Robin worried

about Piglet and Pooh.

He did not know where they were.

He went to the edge of

the water and looked around.

Suddenly, Pooh appeared.

He was floating on a chair.

"Pooh!" cried Christopher Robin.

"I am so glad you are safe!

But where is Piglet?"

Just then something floated out
from under Pooh's chair.
It was a honeypot.

"Here I am," Piglet said

from inside the pot.

"Pooh!" Christopher Robin cried

again. "You saved Piglet!"

"I did?" asked Pooh.

"Yes!" Christopher Robin said.

"You are a hero!"

"I am?" asked Pooh.

"Yes," said Christopher Robin.

"When the storm is over,

I will give you a hero party."

Pooh's hero party had just begun
when Eeyore walked up.

"I found a house for Owl," he said.

"Great!" said Owl. "Where is it?"

"Follow me," said Eeyore.

Everyone followed Eeyore.

Much to their surprise,

when they got to Owl's house

it turned out to be . . .

. . . Piglet's house!

"Why are we stopping here?"

asked Christopher Robin.

"This is Owl's new house,"

Eeyore proudly said.

"What do you think of it?"

Christopher Robin said,

"It is a nice house, Eeyore, but..."

"It is lovely," Kanga added, "but..."

"It is the best house
in the world," Piglet said
with a tear in his eye.

Pooh said quietly to Piglet,

"Tell him it is your house."

"No," Piglet said with a sniff.

"This house belongs to Owl."

"But where will *you* live?" asked Rabbit.

"Well," said Piglet, "I will live..."

"With me!" said Pooh.

"You will live with me,
right, Piglet?"

"Oh, thank you, Pooh," Piglet said.

"Piglet, that was
a great thing to do,"
Christopher Robin said.
"You are a hero!" added Rabbit.

Pooh started to think.

"I am a hero for saving Piglet
in the storm," Pooh said.
"Piglet is a hero for giving
his home to Owl."

"Christopher Robin," Pooh asked,
"can we make a one-hero party
into a two-hero party?"

"Of course we can,"

said Christopher Robin.

And that is just what they did.

Can you match the words with the pictures?

Owl

think

house

party

storm

Fill in the missing letters.

Ee_ore

c_air

h_neypot

Pig_et

_ero

37